ISBN: 978-0-9953434-1-2
Ordering information: Quantity Sales.
Special discounts are available on quantity purchases.
For details email us at:

contact@mouthyprimate.com

Looking For Happiness

Written by Jay Malone
Illustrated by Robert MacDonald

This book is dedicated to Blaze.

On the day I went looking for happiness,
the sky was sunny and blue.

I was looking for something that everyone wants,
but first I needed a clue.

I started by climbing a wall down the street,
and surprised a hive full of bees.

I escaped them by jumping into a pool full of water,
that was instead full of mud and wet leaves.

I climbed up a tree to look near the top,
thinking happiness might be hiding up high.

But all that I found were some eggs and a bird,
who seemed mad that I dared to stop by.

I wanted to stay and make friends with that bird
and see if she could teach me to soar.

But I had to find out where happiness was
so I ran off to go look by the shore.

I found a cool thing in the surf by the dock,
when I stumbled right into a whale!

He couldn't swim off because of a net,
that had wrapped itself up with his tail.

I untangled the line to help him get free,
then asked where he thought I should go.

He answered by shooting me high in the air,
making me think that he just didn't know.

Dark clouds had rolled in and I thought about home,
not wanting to get caught in the cold.

But how do you give up on looking for something,
that's better than a chest full of gold?!

The next place I looked was the forest nearby,
where some bunnies played tag near a rock.

They got startled and ran so I chased them a while,
until mud got all over my sock!

I found some sheep taking a nap on a farm,
and asked if they'd show me the way.

They all got upset and ran back in the barn,
leaving me sneezing and alone on the hay.

The last place I looked was the playground near home,
I asked all of the kids I could see.

They pointed in every direction at once,
so I felt that they knew less than me.

Tired and hungry I walked back to my house,
trying my best not to pout.

Until I thought of one place I'd forgotten,
on the fence where the racoons all hang out!

But it had started to rain and was getting quite dark,
so I decided to head back inside.

I found mom in the kitchen making my favourite food,
and yet all I could do was go hide.

She asked what was wrong and I told her my tale,
telling her all of the places I looked.

She listened in silence with a smile on her face,
only nodding to me as she cooked.

She laughed at me as I sat up in her lap,
and said, "My son you have wasted your day.

The happiness you looked for all over the place,
is just something you feel while you play!"

It's also in all the great things that you love
like pizza, treats and balls.

And in spending time playing games outdoors,
instead of hanging around in malls.

I asked my mom if I could go back outside,
so I could play with my friends or that bird.

But the sun had gone down so she tucked me in bed,
whispering a far greater gift with three words...

I love you.

ABOUT THE AUTHOR

Robert MacDonald went from living & working in Los Angeles
as a comedian, actor & writer under the stage name Jay Malone...

...to living in the middle of the woods back home in Nova Scotia,
Canada with his beautiful wife and three kids under the age of three.

When he's not changing diapers he's blogging about life,
doing standup comedy and self-publishing children's books!

www.MouthyPrimate.com

Join the Email List!

Recieve notifications when new
content becomes available!

www.MouthyPrimate.com

@MouthyPrimate